A Crabtree Branches Book

Let's Go Fish

FLY FISHING

By Kerri Mazzarella

CRABTREE
Publishing Company
www.crabtreebooks.com

School-to-Home Support for Caregivers and Teachers

This high-interest book is designed to motivate striving students with engaging topics while building fluency, vocabulary, and an interest in reading. Here are a few questions and activities to help the reader build upon his or her comprehension skills.

Before Reading:

- *What do I think this book is about?*
- *What do I know about this topic?*
- *What do I want to learn about this topic?*
- *Why am I reading this book?*

During Reading:

- *I wonder why...*
- *I'm curious to know...*
- *How is this like something I already know?*
- *What have I learned so far?*

After Reading:

- *What was the author trying to teach me?*
- *What are some details?*
- *How did the photographs and captions help me understand more?*
- *Read the book again and look for the vocabulary words.*
- *What questions do I still have?*

Extension Activities:

- *What was your favorite part of the book? Write a paragraph on it.*
- *Draw a picture of your favorite thing you learned from the book.*

TABLE OF CONTENTS

WHERE TO FISH

Fly fishing is a type of fishing that includes a rod, reel, line, and fly. It differs from other types of fishing. Fly fishing uses the weight of the line to cast a bait called a fly in to the water.

Fly fishing can be done in fresh and salt waters. Ponds, lakes, streams, and the ocean are great places to fly fish.

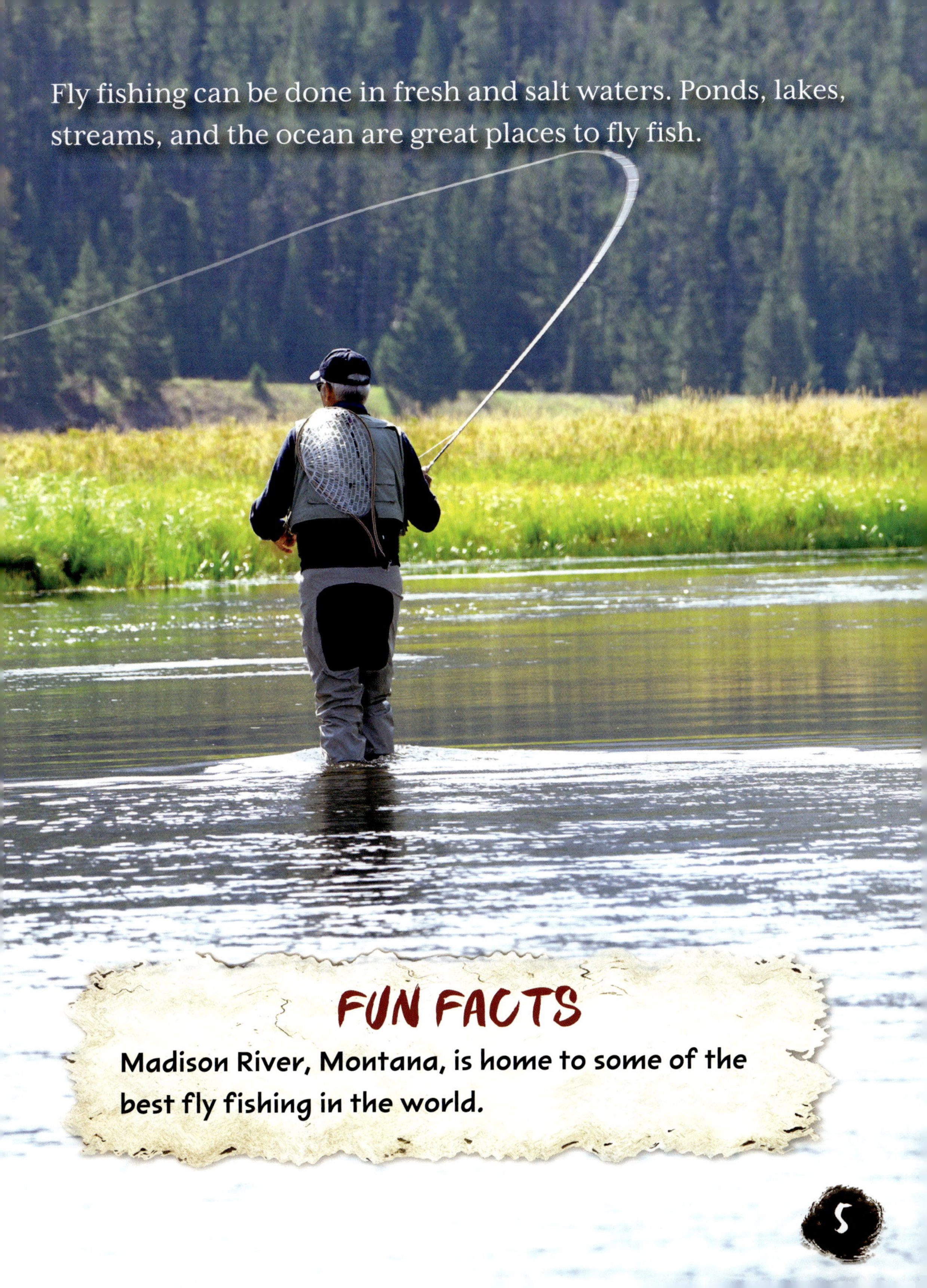

FUN FACTS

Madison River, Montana, is home to some of the best fly fishing in the world.

A special technique is used to cast a fly rod. Casting a fly rod takes practice to master.

Fly fishing can be done in every state across the U.S. Many states have courses or guided trips for beginners.

FUN FACTS

The Florida Keys are home to some of the best saltwater fly fishing in the U.S.

TYPES OF FISH

Many species of fish are caught fly fishing. Both fresh and saltwater fish are exciting to catch.

black crappie panfish

Panfish are popular fish to catch while fly fishing in lakes and ponds. Some are bluegill and bass.

They are a great target for beginner fly fishers.

bluegill

small mouth bass

More experienced fly fishers catch trout, grayling, and salmon in streams and rivers.

king salmon

FUN FACTS

King salmon are a prized catch in Alaska and many fly fishers dream of taking a trip there.

Bonefish, redfish, tarpon, and snook are caught in saltwater areas.

The world record bonefish caught on a fly in the Florida Keys weighed 15.3 pounds (6.9 kg).

SAFETY AND RULES

With any type of fishing, safety is important. When fly fishing, remember to bring a **life jacket** and first aid kit.

Use caution when casting your rod. Fly fishing uses a longer line. Check your surroundings before you cast your hook.

FUN FACTS

Fly fishing can be done on land or by boat.

Some fish have sharp fins that can pierce your skin if they are not handled carefully. When releasing a fish back into the water do this quickly to increase survival of the fish.

snook

In Florida, snook can only be caught in season and must measure between 28 and 32 inches (71 and 81 cm), otherwise they need to be released.

As with all fishing types be sure to purchase a fishing license before you begin fly fishing. These can vary by state or province. Before you begin fly fishing check the rules and size regulations for your area.

RODS AND EQUIPMENT

Fly fishing rods are different than ones used in other types of fishing. Rods are longer, averaging about 9 feet (2.7 m), and are lighter.

You can purchase a beginner fly fishing rod kit for around $150.

Reels are specially designed for a different type of line. **Backing** is the line connected to the reel. It is thick and strong. Fly line is rubbery and heavy and tied to the backing.

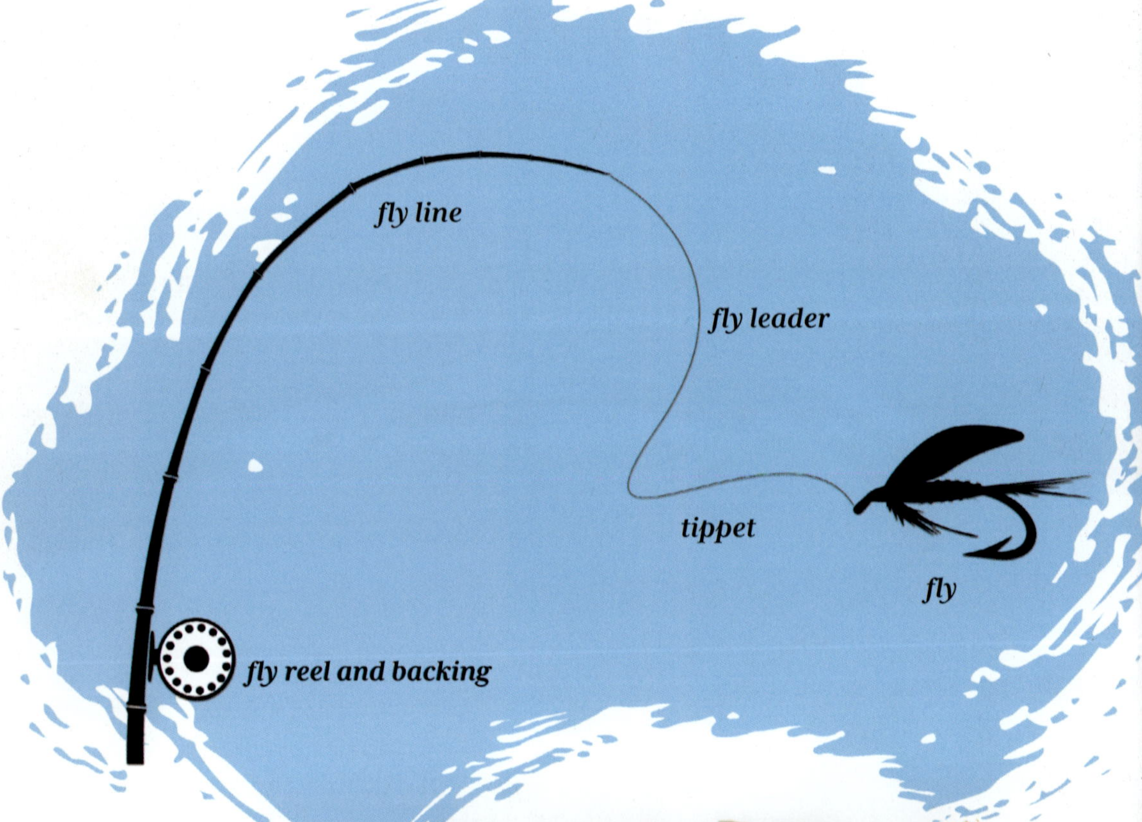

When fly fishing you will also need to be prepared with specific equipment. **Waders** are worn by fly fishers in certain areas. These are important to have and will keep you dry if you are walking into the water.

When fly fishing a **landing net** can be helpful to secure your catch.

WHAT'S IN YOUR TACKLE BOX?

A tackle box used for fly fishing is sometimes called a fly pack. A vest is also a type of tackle box that can be worn.

A fly pack is a small duffle bag that can hold everything you need while fly fishing. This includes spare line, **leaders**, and most importantly your flies.

Some other tackle used for fly fishing are nippers for cutting line and pliers to help release the hook from the mouth of a fish.

pliers

fly fishing multi tool

Wearing a fly fishing vest makes it easy to grab any tackle you might need while standing out in the water.

You can purchase a fly fishing vest for around $40.

TYPES OF BAIT

Fly fishing is known for its use of a specific bait. **Artificial flies** are the bait used in this type of fishing. A **tippet** is line that the fly is tied to.

There are thousands of types of flies to choose from. Flies are made from colorful furs, feathers, or other material fastened around a hook. You can buy bait for fly fishing, or you can make your own. Many people enjoy making flies at home.

You can purchase a beginners assortment of flies for around $35.

There are three types of artificial baits used that are like food fish normally eat.

Dry flies float and mimic insects. Nymphs also mimic insects but sink. Streamers sink and mimic baitfish.

dry fly

nymph

streamer

Fly fishing is a great way to connect with nature and enjoy the outdoors. Remember, with fly fishing practice makes perfect!

GLOSSARY

artificial flies (ahr-tuh-FISH-uhl flies): Artificial bait that looks like a fly normally consisting of feathers or fur tied around a special hook

backing (BAK-ing): The thick line used for fighting fish that is attached to a fly fishing reel

bonefish (BOHN-fish): A silvery gamefish of warm coastal waters

fly fishing (flahy FISH-ing): The sport of fishing using a rod and artificial fly as bait

landing net (LAN-ding net): A small bag-shaped net with a handle at the mouth, used for scooping a hooked fish out of the water

leader (LEE-der): Clear fishing line attached to fly fishing line while fly fishing

life jacket (lahyf JAK-it): A sleeveless buoyant or inflatable jacket for keeping a person afloat in water

panfish (PAN-fish): A fish suitable for frying whole in a pan, especially one caught by an angler

tippet (TIP-it): A thin clear line attached to the leader in fly fishing. An artificial fly is attached to the tippet.

waders (WEY-derz): High waterproof boots or a waterproof garment for the legs and body, used especially by anglers while fishing

INDEX

WEBSITES TO VISIT

www.takemefishing.org/fly-fishing/fly-fishing-basics/fly-fishing-for-beginners/

www.flylordsmag.com

www.hikingandfishing.com

ABOUT THE AUTHOR

Kerri Mazzarella was raised on the East coast of Southern Florida. She enjoys all types of fishing. Her family spends the weekends on their boat catching fish in the river and ocean. Her two sons are experienced fly fishers. Although Kerri has not fly fished before, she has helped make artificial flies with her boys.

CRABTREE Publishing Company

Written by: Kerri Mazzarella
Designed by: Kathy Walsh
Proofreader: Crystal Sikkens

Photographs: Shutterstock; Cover: ©Paul Winterman, ©MicroOne, ©Zerbor, ©GreyMoth; Pg 3, 4, 8, 12, 17, 21, 26 © ESB professional; Pg 1, 3, 8, 10, 13, 16, 19, 20, 22, 26 © MicroOne; Pg 5, 7, 10, 13 ©Zerbor; Pg 4 ©goodluz; Pg 6 ©Theunis Jacobus Botha; Pg 7 ©The Floridian; Pg 8 ©M Huston; Pg 9 ©CSNafzger; Pg 10 ©Marc Cappelletti; Pg 11 ©DUSAN ZIDAR; Pg 12 ©e-leet; Pg 13 ©goodluz; Pg 14 ©wwwarjag, ©CaptJason; Pg 16 ©usfara /2pixabay; Pg 17 ©GROGL; Pg 18 ©Marc Cappelletti, ©Sandra Cunningham; Pg 19 ©Estrada Anton; Pg 20 ©goodluz; Pg 21 ©Earl D. Walker; Pg 22 ©Christine Glade; Pg 23 ©VidEst; Pg 25 ©lauraslens; Pg 26 ©ivosar; Pg 27 ©Jason Gillman from Pixabay; Pg 28 ©Lane V. Erickson, ©David W. Leindecker, ©Tyler Hulett, ©Shane W Thompson

Library and Archives Canada Cataloguing in Publication
CIP available at Library and Archives Canada

Library of Congress Cataloging-in-Publication Data
CIP available at Library of Congress

Crabtree Publishing Company
www.crabtreebooks.com 1-800-387-7650

Printed in the USA/072022/CG20220201

Published in the United States Crabtree Publishing
347 Fifth Avenue, Suite 1402-145
New York, NY, 10016

Published in Canada Crabtree Publishing
616 Welland Ave.
St. Catharines, Ontario L2M 5V6